The Case Of The
High Seas Secret

Look for more great books in

series:

The Case Of The
High Seas Secret

by Alice Leonhardt

📖HarperEntertainment
An Imprint of HarperCollinsPublishers

A PARACHUTE PRESS BOOK

PARACHUTE
PRESS

Parachute Publishing, L.L.C.
156 Fifth Avenue
New York, NY 10010

DUALSTAR
PUBLICATIONS

Dualstar Publications
c/o Thorne and Company
A Professional Law Corporation
1801 Century Park East
Los Angeles, CA 90067

HarperEntertainment

An Imprint of HarperCollins*Publishers*
10 East 53rd Street, New York, NY 10022

outta site!
mary-kateandashley.com™
Register Now

1

OLSENS AHOY!

"**D**o you feel like we forgot something?" I asked my twin sister, Ashley.

We walked up the crowded gangplank of the *Jolly Roger* cruise ship. Our whole family was going on a Caribbean cruise.

"No, Mary-Kate, I remembered everything," Ashley said. "Sunblock, bathing suits, snorkel, books—"

I shouldn't have asked. My sister is *very* organized. Me, I just threw some stuff into my suitcase.

"What else do you need on a cruise?" Ashley asked.

"How about an eye patch?" I suggested.

"An eye patch?" Ashley gave me a funny look.

I pointed to the man shaking hands with our little sister, Lizzie. He had a droopy mustache and long black hair. A gold earring dangled from his ear. A feather was sticking up from his three-cornered hat. And a leather patch covered one eye.

"The name of our ship is the *Jolly Roger*," I hinted.

"Oh, right." Ashley nodded. "This whole cruise has a pirate theme."

"Welcome aboard, mateys!" The man with the earring grabbed my hand.

"I'm Captain Teach!" he boomed. "My crew and I are here to make sure you have a wonderful trip. If you don't, then it's off with your heads!" He made a slicing motion along his neck with his fingers.

"Eek!" Lizzie squealed and jumped back.

"He's just pretending, Lizzie," Ashley said. She patted Lizzie's shoulder.

Captain Teach laughed. Then he lifted up his eye patch and winked. "I *am* just pretending. But we do want you all to have a wonderful time." He grinned, showing fake rotten teeth.

Gross. Ashley, Lizzie, and I hurried to catch up with Mom, Dad, and Trent, our big brother. They were talking to a teenage girl with short blond hair. She was dressed in a pirate's costume.

She didn't have rotten teeth or an eye patch. But she did have a parrot! It perched on her shoulder, staring at us with its black beady eyes.

"Hi, I'm Georgina." The girl smiled. "Captain Teach is my dad. And this is Peter Pan." She nodded toward the bird.

"Peter want a cracker?" I chirped.

Peter ruffled his wings. He had blue and

green feathers and a long tail.

"If that's Peter Pan, are you Captain Hook?" Lizzie asked the girl.

Georgina held up her hand and wiggled her fingers. "Nope. See, no hook."

"So what do you do on the ship?" I asked Georgina.

"I help out with special events for kids," Georgina explained. "In fact, we have a lot of fun stuff planned at Captain Kidd's Corner. That's the recreation room. Hope to see you there."

"Ashley and I are ready for some fun," I said.

"Good. Today and tomorrow we're having a super scavenger hunt." Georgina handed each of us a chocolate coin wrapped in gold paper. "Have a doubloon."

"We're rich!" Peter squawked in Georgina's ear.

Georgina winced. "See you guys at Captain Kidd's Corner at two o'clock," she said as she walked away.

SCREECH!

A high, sharp noise made me jump. Then something dropped on my head. Something furry with sharp claws and a long tail.

"Yikes!" I cried. "Get it off me!"

2

PERFECT PARTNERS

"**H**elp!" I shouted, jumping up and down. The furry thing hung on tight.

My family burst out laughing.

"Mary-Kate, it's only a monkey," Ashley said.

I stopped jumping and shouting. *What? A monkey?*

The animal dropped onto my shoulder. Then he grabbed the gold coin from my hand and scampered down the deck.

"Hey!" I hollered. Ashley and I chased

the monkey. He ran to Captain Teach. Then he climbed up Captain Teach's leg and leaped onto the captain's head. He perched on the captain's hat and chattered at us.

"Your monkey took my doubloon," I told the captain.

He laughed. "That's Calico Jack," he said. "He's our ship mascot. Give the money back, Jack."

The monkey tossed the gold coin to the floor. I picked it up. Yuck. Teeth marks had broken the foil. So much for my tasty treat.

"Say you're sorry, Jack," Captain Teach said.

The monkey leaned down. He stretched out his hand.

I shook his tiny paw. "He really is cute," I admitted.

"Come on, Mary-Kate." Ashley tapped my shoulder. "We need to catch up with Mom and Dad."

Ashley and I hurried to the main

entrance hall. It looked like a jungle. Potted palm trees lined the walls. Beautiful plants hung from the ceiling.

We found Mom, Dad, Lizzie, and Trent studying a map of the ship.

"This is the upper deck," Mom told us. "Our cabins are U68 and U70. Why don't we go find them?"

A young man greeted us when we reached our cabins. He wore a blue-and-white striped shirt and baggy pants. Around his waist was a black sash. Around his neck was a red bandanna.

"Are you a pirate, too?" Lizzie asked him.

"I am your cabin steward, Timothy," he said, smiling. "I will tend to your rooms and get you anything you need during the trip. Your suitcases are already in your cabins."

Ashley and I were going to share cabin U68. "This is so cool!" I said when we went inside the small room. "Everything in here is so tiny. Mini–bunk beds, mini-dresser, minidesk, minichair."

"Even a teensy bathroom," Ashley added.

"I get the top bunk!" I called. I quickly climbed up the ladder on the side of the bed. There were rails so you wouldn't fall out when the ship rolled.

Ashley opened the window. "The ship is almost ready to leave," she said. "Let's go up on deck and wave goodbye."

"Who will we wave to?" I asked.

"To everybody watching!" Ashley replied.

When we reached the deck, it was filled with people. Some threw colored streamers. Others waved to the crowd on the dock.

Ashley and I leaned over the railing and waved, too. *"Bon voyage!"* people called back to us. That means "have a good trip" in French. It's a tradition to say it.

Next to us stood a red-haired girl about

our age. Only she looked a lot older because she wore makeup and a pink suit. She was throwing kisses to a group of girls on the dock.

The girls on the dock were screaming, "We love you Danielle!" One of them held up a sign that said: WE'LL MISS YOU, GABBY GUMSHOE.

I nudged Ashley. "That's Danielle Defoe. You know, from the TV show, *Gabby Gumshoe*."

Ashley peered over at her. "It sure is. She's pretty hard to miss."

Just then another girl shoved her way to the railing beside us. She had brown braids and glasses.

"Danielle Defoe! Is it really *you*?" The girl gasped.

Danielle frowned. "Do I know you?"

"I'm Molly Ferris. President of the Gabby Gumshoe Fan Club! I can't believe I'm on the same ship with you!"

"Me neither," Danielle said. "Sorry. I've got to go now." She turned and walked away.

Molly's shoulders slumped. "Bye," she called after Danielle. "Nice to meet you."

"That was so rude," I whispered to Ashley.

TOOOOT. TOOT.

The ship's horn blasted as it pulled away from the dock.

"Time for the scavenger hunt," Ashley said. "Let's go!"

The *Jolly Roger* cruise ship had nine decks. We had to climb four flights of stairs to get to Captain Kidd's Corner. It was a big recreation room near the outdoor pool.

"Awesome!" I exclaimed when I opened the door. The room was filled with games and craft projects. In the middle of the room was a huge pirate ship. Its mast rose to the ceiling. Some kids were climbing up the rope rigging. Others fought on deck with rubber swords. Two boys were shooting a pretend cannon.

"This looks almost real," I said to Ashley as we climbed up the gangplank. Then we heard a sharp whistle blast.

Georgina was on the deck, waving. Captain Teach stood beside her.

"Time for the scavenger hunt!" Georgina called.

Everyone hurried to gather around her. I counted thirteen kids, including Molly Ferris. Then I spotted Danielle coming into the room. A boy who looked about nine tagged along after her. I figured he had to be Danielle's brother. He had the same wavy red hair and freckles.

Danielle was wearing shorts now, so she looked more like a normal kid. Except for her grumpy expression.

Molly eagerly ran over to stand next to her.

"Okay, everybody. Here are the rules,"

Georgina said. "Each team gets three clues. They'll take you all over the ship."

Danielle started to yawn. She quickly covered her mouth.

"Each team will get different clues that lead to different prizes," Georgina went on. "And with each prize you will get a new clue. The team that finds all three of their prizes first wins!"

"Wins what?" Danielle asked in a bored voice.

Georgina grinned. "A trip to Adventure Island!"

"Adventure Island!" I gasped. "Isn't that the cool new theme park opening in San Diego?"

Ashley squealed. "It's supposed to have the fastest rides ever!"

All the kids were buzzing with excitement. Even Danielle didn't look so bored now.

Georgina blew her whistle again. "The

winners and their parents will be the first to visit the park," she added when we all got quiet. "Sound like fun?"

"Yes!" everybody yelled.

"Okay. Now listen up," Georgina went on. "That means you must bring all three prizes and all three clues to the recreation room by three o'clock sharp tomorrow to win."

"What if everyone finds all three of their prizes?" I asked.

Captain Teach smiled broadly. "Well then," he said. "I guess we'll just give the trip to Georgina for doing such a good job."

"Dad!" Georgina protested, nudging him. She turned back to us. "Then we'll have a tiebreaker clue," she said. "So let's get started. Gather into teams of two. I guess we'll need one team of three since we have an odd number of kids."

Ashley and I quickly grabbed each other's hands. Molly latched on to Danielle.

"Danielle, can I be on your team?"

Danielle's brother asked her. "I know a lot about boats."

"Yeah, maybe the ones you play with in the bathtub," Danielle said. "No way, Oliver."

"You can join our team, Oliver," Ashley called.

"Sure," I added. "The more the merrier."

Oliver stared at us. Then his jaw dropped. "Hey, you're the Trenchcoat Twins!"

Molly sniffed. "Who are the Trenchcoat Twins?"

"They're *real* detectives," Oliver said. "I read about them in *Cool Kids* magazine."

"Are you two as good as Danielle?" Molly asked.

Ashley and I looked at each other. We didn't want to point out the obvious.

"Danielle? A detective?" Oliver burst out laughing. "The Trenchcoat Twins solve *real* mysteries. Danielle solves fake ones."

Danielle put her hands on her hips.

"Who are you calling a fake, you worm?"

"Don't worry about them, Danielle," Molly said. "We'll show them who's the best. We'll win the scavenger hunt!"

Danielle finally looked at her and smiled. "With our eyes closed," she added. The two flounced off.

By now all of the other teams had left Captain Kidd's Corner.

Oliver sighed. "My sister used to be nice," he told us. "But she turned into a big pain when she became a star. Thanks for asking me to join your team."

Ashley grinned. "No problem. It'll be fun. And Mary-Kate and I are pretty good at solving clues."

Oliver brightened. "That's right. With your clue-solving skills, and all I know about boats, we might even win."

"You will *never* win," an eerie voice cackled behind us.

"The treasure is MINE!"

3

FOOD FOR THOUGHT

We spun around. Peter Pan, that noisy parrot, was perched on a lantern above our heads.

Georgina hurried over to us and shook her head. "He's been on this ship so long listening to pirate-talk that he sounds like a pirate himself," she said.

She handed me a folded piece of paper. "Okay, guys. Here's your team's first clue. Remember, no treasure hunting during dinner or after eight-thirty," she added.

I read the clue aloud:

"This was a name for a sailing ship. And it is also a place where hungry pirates would look for a special treat!"

Ashley frowned. "Huh? What does that mean?"

"That's an easy one," Oliver said, shrugging. "It's a galley. A kind of ship that was used a long time ago. It's also the name for a ship's kitchen."

"Wow, Oliver. You really do know all about boats," I said, impressed.

"We're going to win for sure," Ashley said. "Come on, let's go!"

The three of us raced out of Captain Kidd's Corner. Ashley found a crew member in the hallway. "Excuse me. Could you tell me where the ship's galley is?" she asked.

"It's on the dining deck, young lady." He

directed us to the stairs. "Two levels down. Walk through the main dining room. Then go through the double doors."

It took a while, but we finally found the galley. We pushed open the double doors. Then we stopped in our tracks. The ship's galley was larger than the inside of our house!

Oliver groaned. "There's no way we'll find any prize in here."

"Welcome, welcome, little buccaneers!" One of the cooks rushed up, waving a wooden spoon. He wore a white apron and a chef's hat. "You want a tour?"

"Yes, please. We're *hungry pirates*," Ashley said. "Looking for a *special treat*."

"Right." I nodded. Ashley was repeating the words from the clue on purpose.

But the cook didn't seem to notice. He led the way through the busy galley. "The *Jolly Roger* has twenty cooks," he told us. "We fix three meals and four snacks a day."

Yum. But what would hungry pirates want for an extra-special treat? Then it hit me. *Fruit!*

At school we learned about sailors on long voyages. Fresh fruit was hard to keep. And the sailors sucked on lemons for vitamin C so they wouldn't get sick.

Just then the cook stopped in front of a counter. On it was a bowl of oranges, lemons, and apples.

The cook's eyes twinkled. As if he knew a secret!

"A special treat for a hungry pirate!" I exclaimed. I reached into the bowl. My fingers wrapped around something small and hard. I pulled it out. It was a golden apple.

Oliver punched the air with his fist. "Yes! Our first prize!"

"Good thinking, Mary-Kate," Ashley said. She reached into the bowl, too—and pulled out the second clue.

The cook smiled. "Looks like it's time for

you to go," he said. We thanked him for the tour. Then we went back into the main dining hall. Waiters were setting the tables.

"It's almost dinnertime," Ashley said.

"So we're not allowed to hunt anymore," I said. "Georgina's rule, remember?"

Oliver shrugged. "That's okay. That tour of the galley made me hungry."

"Let's just read our second clue then," Ashley said. "We can think about the answer at dinner." She unfolded the paper and read aloud:

"This is something that helps you reach land. But if you 'look' for the captain here, he'll help you 'see' your next prize!"

I frowned, totally puzzled. Oliver was scratching his head. Ashley was tapping her lip.

"I'll think better after I eat," Oliver said.

"What cabin are you guys in?"

"We're in U68," Ashley said. "On the upper deck."

"My family's in U59, so that's pretty near you," Oliver said. "We have one of the big cabins." He rolled his eyes. "For the *big* star, you know."

We headed upstairs so we could get ready for dinner.

"Where should we stash the booty?" Oliver asked.

"Stash the *booty*?" I grinned. "Is that pirate talk for loot? Soon you'll be wearing a pirate eye patch, too."

"Let's put the prize in our cabin," Ashley suggested. "It'll be safe there."

When we reached the upper deck, we hurried down the hall. Danielle and Molly were just coming around the corner.

"Guess what, Gabby the Not-So-Great Detective?" Oliver bragged to his sister. "We found our first prize."

Molly's mouth fell open. Danielle's eyes narrowed. "So what!" She marched into the cabin, slamming the door in Oliver's face.

"Gosh, you sure made her mad," Molly said. She shook her head and walked off down the hall. Ashley and I said goodbye to Oliver. Then we went into our cabin.

"I'll put the golden apple and the clue with my hair clips," I told Ashley. I opened the lid of my wooden box and carefully placed them inside.

We changed into sundresses for dinner. Then we found Mom, Dad, and Lizzie. Trent was sitting with a bunch of boys. Their table was pretty loud.

Dinner was really yummy. We'd never seen so much great food in one place. There was even a huge buffet table filled with every kind of dessert you could imagine.

After dinner we walked over to Georgina's table. She was sitting with a group of older kids. And this time she was dressed in a Tinker Bell costume. She wore light green tights and a green belted tunic. Wings hung from her back.

"To go with that crazy parrot Peter Pan," she explained. "Dad thought it would be cute." But she sounded as if she didn't think it was cute at all.

Soon some kids from the other teams came up to talk to Georgina, too. Molly and Danielle were still eating dinner. It looked as if Oliver, Ashley, and I were the only ones who had found our first prize.

"Wow," Georgina said. She tapped Oliver's head playfully with her wand. "You three are quick. I'll have to keep my eye on you. Otherwise, I'll have to give away that terrific prize way too fast."

"They're not *that* quick!" Molly said, hurrying over with Danielle. Molly held up a bag of gold doubloons.

"We found our first prize, too," Danielle said. She inspected her fingernails, as if finding a prize was no big deal.

"Gabby Gumshoe is the *best* detective," Molly went on, "in the *world*. And we're going to win."

"Well, it looks like a tie so far," Georgina said, smiling. "Did you figure out your second clues?"

"It will be *sooo* easy," Danielle said, shrugging.

Oliver scowled. "Come on," he said to Ashley and me. "Let's find that second prize."

"Oops. I left the clue back in our room with the apple," I said.

"That's okay," Oliver said. "I need to change anyway."

When Ashley and I walked into our cabin, our mouths fell open. What a mess! My beach hat and sunglasses were tossed on the floor. My wooden box was on the floor, too. Scrunchies, clips, and hair bands were scattered everywhere.

I groaned. "What happened? I didn't leave it this way."

Ashley shrugged. "It was probably the rolling of the ship."

I dropped to my knees and began picking up the stuff. Then I stopped and frowned. "Ashley, I don't see the apple!"

"That's weird." Ashley bent over and checked under the bed. We searched all over the room. But our prize had totally disappeared!

"I wish Clue was here to sniff out that apple." I sighed. Clue was our basset hound. She helped us solve mysteries sometimes.

Ashley snapped her fingers. "Wait. Maybe it rolled into the bathroom."

She dashed into the bathroom. "M-M-Mary-Kate!" she stammered a second later. "Look what was taped to our mirror."

She held out a piece of torn, faded paper.

"Ooo." Gingerly I took the paper. There

was writing all over it in some kind of red ink. The letters were splotchy and still wet.

I read the message out loud. "You'll walk the plank before YOU get the treasure!"

4

I Spy...

"Walk the plank?" Ashley repeated. "Isn't that how pirates made their enemies jump off the boat into the ocean? Someone must be trying to scare us!"

"Danielle and Molly," I guessed. Then my eyes widened. "Hey, I bet those guys took our apple, too!"

"We don't have any proof of that," Ashley said. "Besides, how would they have gotten into the cabin?"

I shook my head. "Beats me. But it looks

like this scavenger hunt is turning into a real mystery!"

"I still think the apple is around here somewhere," Ashley said. "It probably rolled into a corner."

"Well, *I* think somebody took it," I said. "The same somebody who left this creepy message." I touched the damp writing. Then I sniffed my finger. "Marker. Who would have red markers on the ship?"

"There was art stuff in the recreation room," Ashley mumbled from under the bed.

"Knock, knock." Oliver peered into the cabin. "Hey, why are you crawling around on the floor, Ashley?"

"She's being a detective," I said.

"Cool!" Oliver went over to the bed and got down on his hands and knees. "Uh, what are we looking for?"

I gulped. "The golden apple."

He jerked up. "What! Our first prize is missing?"

I nodded. "But we still have our second clue."

"Oh, boy," Oliver grumbled. "Now I'm never going to beat my sister."

"Sure you will, Oliver," Ashley said. "But even if you don't, you may get to solve a *real* mystery."

Oliver smiled. "Hey, I didn't think of that."

I handed him the nasty warning about the plank.

"Gross," Oliver said, holding the paper away. "Where did you find this?"

When I told him, he nodded. "I bet my stupid sister wrote it. She and Molly will do anything to win. Gabby Gumshoe's reputation is at stake."

Ashley stood up. "Maybe. But detectives never jump to conclusions."

Ashley strapped her fanny pack around her waist. Then she pulled out her pad and pen. "Okay, team, let's go. It's time to figure out who left that message."

We marched into the hall and found our cabin steward. He was folding towels on a cart.

"Timothy, did anyone go into our cabin?" I asked him.

"I did not see anyone, miss," he said.

"Who else has a key?" Ashley asked.

He shrugged. "Besides your family? Me. And the purser has a master key."

"What's a purser?" I asked.

"He's the manager of the ship," Timothy explained. "His name is Mr. Banim."

Ashley wrote down the name. "Thanks, Timothy."

When the steward left Ashley said, "I think we need to talk to Mr. Banim."

"Why don't we find our second prize first?" Oliver said.

"Okay, good idea," Ashley said, nodding. "We can find Mr. Banim later."

She took out the second clue and read it out loud again:

"This is something that helps you reach land. But if you 'look' for the captain here, he'll help you 'see' your next prize!"

Oliver poked one finger in the air. "I know the answer! It's the bridge. But not like the kind over water, though. The place where the captain works is called a bridge, too."

"Awesome!" Ashley cried.

I put an arm around Oliver's shoulders. "We're really glad you're on our team, Oliver," I said.

This time we had to climb five flights of stairs. On our way up we ran into Tony and Dell, two kids from another team. They were walking down the stairs, frowning.

"What's wrong?" Ashley asked them.

"We lost our second prize," Dell said. "A little gold treasure chest. I put it in my pocket, but now it's gone."

"And you know Susan and Karl?" Tony put in. "After dinner they found a silver globe. Susan had it in her backpack. That disappeared, too."

My brows shot up. Ashley and I looked at each other. *What was going on here?*

Ashley whipped out her pad and pen. I told Tony and Dell about our missing apple. Ashley made notes about the other missing prizes.

"We still have our first prize," Tony said. He pulled it out of his pocket. It was a tiny carved boat. "I guess the thief didn't want this one."

Oliver tugged on my sleeve. "Come on. We've got to hurry and find our second prize," he whispered.

"We'll keep our eyes peeled for the lost prizes," I told Tony and Dell. Then I nudged Ashley and we hurried after Oliver.

Huffing and puffing, we finally reached the bridge. It was just a small room with windows, but from the window we could see the whole ship.

"Cool," I said.

"Ahoy, mateys!" a voice called. A tall man came toward us. It was Captain Teach! But he looked totally different. He was in his fancy captain's uniform. And he didn't have long hair, or an eye patch, or rotten teeth.

"Ahoy, Captain." Oliver shook his hand.

"Have you come for a tour of the bridge?" the captain asked, smiling. He waved his hand. The room was filled with computers and panels of switches and lights. "From here I run the *Jolly Roger*."

"We came to *see* what you do," I said.

Ashley was wandering around the room, tapping her lip. I could tell she was trying to figure out what our second prize might be.

The captain went over to one of the observation windows. He picked up a telescope. "Look through here," he told me. "Tell me what you see."

I held it to one eye. In the distance I could see rows of lights. "It's another boat!" I said.

"Wait a minute!" Ashley said suddenly. She turned to Oliver and me. "I know what the next prize is. *Look* for the captain. He'll help you *see* your next prize."

Oliver took the telescope from me. "This is it! Our prize is his telescope. Awesome." He peered through it.

The captain chuckled. "I'm afraid not, young man. Not this telescope. But maybe you'll find a smaller one."

We searched and searched. The whole time Captain Teach grinned heartily. He knew where the prize was, I could tell.

Finally Ashley spotted it. A tiny silver telescope was peeking out from the band of the captain's hat. Captain Teach handed it to her.

"Don't forget the next clue, sir," Oliver reminded him.

"Oh, right." The captain winked. "You three *are* good detectives." He took off his hat. A piece of paper was tucked inside it. He gave the clue to Oliver. "If the ship gets lost, I'll call on you for help."

Just as Oliver was about to respond to the captain, the loudspeaker crackled. "All right, young pirates," Georgina's voice announced. "It's eight-thirty. No more scavenger hunting until after breakfast tomorrow morning."

Ashley, Oliver, and I all groaned. We'd run out of time!

"And remember, everyone," Georgina's voice continued. "You're all on pirate's honor. Good night, mateys!"

The loudspeaker clicked off.

Ashley sighed. "Well, that's it, I guess."

We thanked Captain Teach and left the bridge. Ashley carefully placed the clue and the telescope inside her jeans pocket. I saw her push them down deep.

"I'm not taking any chances," she said.

"Good idea," I said. Then I yawned. "Maybe it's time to call it a night."

Oliver seemed a little disappointed as we headed back to our cabins. When we reached our hallway, we saw Molly heading toward us. She had a smug look on her face.

"Guess what? Danielle and I have our first and second prizes," she boasted. "A treasure map and a bag of those chocolate doubloons. So *now* who are the best detectives?"

"We are," Oliver shot right back. "We're on the trail of a *real* mystery. A mystery that you and Gabby the fake-o detective would never be able to solve."

"Don't you call Danielle a fake." Molly shook her finger in Oliver's face.

I sucked in my breath.

Molly had a smudge of something red on her hand. And it was the same color as the mysterious message we'd found in our room!

DUSTING FOR CLUES

I poked Ashley with my elbow. She was staring at Molly's hand, too.

"Hey, Molly, you'd better wash your hand," Ashley told her. "Before you get that red stuff on your clothes."

Molly frowned at her hand. "Oh, it's just marker. I was signing autographs for Danielle."

"Why? Did she forget how to spell her name?" Oliver joked.

"No," Molly shot back. "She was just tired."

"Shouldn't *Danielle* sign the autographs?" I asked. "Isn't that the whole point?"

Molly crossed her arms. "Even ace detectives need a break once in a while," she told us.

That's for sure, I thought.

Just then, Oliver's mother opened the door to their suite. "Oliver, time for bed," she called.

Oliver headed toward the door. "Don't forget," he whispered. "We have to look for the apple soon." Then he slipped inside his cabin.

When the door closed, I turned toward Ashley. "So what do you think?"

"Well, Molly's explanation sort of made sense," Ashley said. "She may have been telling the truth."

"But if she didn't write the message, who did?" I asked.

Ashley pulled out her pad. "I think we

have some serious detective work to do before we hit the sack. Still sleepy?"

I shook my head. "Not when we have missing prizes to track down. And we have to figure out who left that creepy message."

"Then let's go find Mr. Banim," Ashley said. "The first thing we need to know is who else can enter our cabin."

We went downstairs to the purser's desk. We found it next to the ship's beauty parlor. A tired-looking man behind the desk was listening to a complaining passenger. I read the man's nametag: R. BANIM.

"My bed's lumpy and the pillows are hard," the woman was saying. She wore a fuzzy bathrobe and she looked almost as tired as Mr. Banim.

A shrill screech made me whirl around. Calico Jack was swinging from a hanging plant. "Hey, Jack. What are you doing here?" I called.

The monkey climbed down a vine and

dropped on the counter. "Eek!" the woman screamed. "Get that…that *thing* away from me."

Jack chattered at her. Then he jumped into Ashley's arms.

The tired woman gave Jack a disgusted look, and rushed off.

"Hey, Jack, you scamp." Mr. Banim laughed. "Are you ready to go in your cage for the night?"

Jack chattered angrily. Then he hopped from Ashley's arms and scampered down the hall.

The purser sighed. "Now I'll never catch him."

"Mr. Banim, we were wondering who might have a key to our cabin," Ashley said.

Mr. Banim glanced at us. "Why? Is there a problem?" he asked.

"No, not at all," I said quickly. "We're just…doing a little research on the *Jolly Roger*."

"For our scavenger hunt," Ashley added.

Mr. Banim looked up our cabin number in a big book. "Well, let's see. You, your parents, the cabin steward, and me," Mr. Banim said. "That's it."

I watched as Ashley quickly scribbled the names in her notebook.

"Oh, yes," Mr. Banim added suddenly. "I almost forgot. Georgina, the captain's daughter, needed to get into your room earlier. For the scavenger hunt, I believe."

My eyes widened. Ashley stopped making notes on her pad.

Did Georgina sneak into our room to leave the plank warning? Did *she* take the golden apple? And if she did, why?

Ashley and I thanked Mr. Banim. Then we walked back downstairs.

"Can you believe that?" Ashley said. "Georgina was in our room!"

"So that makes her a suspect," I said.

"Actually, anyone who could get into the

room could be a suspect," Ashley pointed out. "Don't forget Timothy and Mr. Banim."

"But neither of them has a motive," I said. A motive is a person's reason for committing a crime.

"Well, okay. What would Georgina's motive be?" Ashley asked.

"The captain said that if no one solved the scavenger hunt, then he'd give Georgina the trip to Adventure Island!" I reminded my sister. "She's the culprit. Case closed."

"Hold the phone, Mary-Kate," Ashley said. "We don't have enough proof to say that for sure."

I pointed to a blond girl in a Tinker Bell costume coming out of a door marked "Staff Room." "Well, there she is. Let's follow her."

Georgina moved pretty fast. But we tailed her all over the ship. Finally, she ducked into the movie theater. It was totally dark. And we lost track of our suspect until

I spotted something sparkly on the carpet.

"Fairy dust," I whispered to Ashley. We followed the trail through the theater and out the exit. We ran up stairs and down corridors. Then the fairy dust disappeared. And so had Georgina.

We stopped to catch our breath. Now we were in a dark, narrow hall.

"I think we're lost," I told Ashley.

Ashley pulled a map of the *Jolly Roger* from her backpack. "I bet we're right here," she said, pointing. "We turned left back at the arcade."

"Nope," I cut in. "We turned right. And then—OUCH!"

Ashley's fingernails were digging into my arm. She was staring straight ahead.

I followed my sister's gaze. On the wall in front of us was a creepy black shadow.

My heart thumped. Slowly I turned around. Someone was hiding in the stairwell—waiting for us!

NOW YOU SEE IT,
NOW YOU DON'T

"**W**ho do you think that is?" I asked nervously. The shadow wasn't very big. But before Ashley could answer, the shadow disappeared!

Ashley and I raced up the stairwell and onto the deck.

No one was there. We were standing in front of a row of covered lifeboats.

Ashley sighed. "Well, whoever it was is gone," she said. "I didn't even hear footsteps."

"Well, they sure didn't jump overboard." I glanced over the railing. I could hear the water moving below. But it was too far down and too dark to see anything.

I shivered. "There's no way someone would jump off this ship and swim," she said.

"Where do you think the person went?" Ashley asked.

"I don't know," I answered. "But I need to check something. Let's go back to the hall. I want do a little experiment."

Ashley followed me to the exit door. The ship rose and fell on the waves. Something rolled under my feet. I stooped and picked it up. It was a silver globe.

I held it up. "Hey, this must be the prize Susan and Karl lost!" I said excitedly.

Ashley nodded. "The thief must have dropped it," she said.

When we reached the hall, I tried my experiment. I stood in the stairwell so

Ashley couldn't see me. She was standing back in the hall.

"So what does my shadow look like?" I called to my sister.

"It's the same size as the shadow our mystery person made," Ashley said slowly. "Which means the thief is a kid."

"But watch this, Ashley," I said. I stepped forward, then backward.

"The shadow is changing size," Ashley called. "What's going on?"

I stepped back into the hall. Ashley looked puzzled.

"The size of the shadow changed when I moved," I explained. "So that means our thief could have been tall *or* short."

Ashley sighed. "Then we can't rule out anyone. It still could be Georgina."

"Don't forget Molly or Danielle," I added, "or any of the other kids." Then I yawned. I couldn't help it.

That made Ashley yawn, too. She pulled

out her map again. "We'd better find our way back to our cabin," she said. "Before Mom and Dad get worried."

"Besides," I added, "we need to get our rest. I get the feeling tomorrow is going to be a long day."

The next morning Oliver knocked on our door. Hard. "All hands on deck!" he hollered.

Ashley and I both groaned. We had decided to stay up really late last night and search our room for the golden apple. That wasn't cheating since we'd already found the prize once. But we didn't have any luck this time.

Oliver banged again. "Come on, guys! It's almost nine o'clock! Time to start looking for our third prize!"

That got us out of bed. We dressed in a flash. Ashley strapped on her fanny pack. We ran out into the hall.

Oliver was leaning against the wall,

frowning. "It's about time."

"We're sorry, Oliver," Ashley said. "But we looked all over our room and we didn't find the apple. Maybe we should start—"

"Ahhhh!" someone shouted.

"That sounded like it came from your cabin," I said to Oliver.

We all turned around just as Danielle flung open the door. Molly was right behind her. "Our bag of doubloons is gone!" Danielle screamed. She reached out and grabbed Oliver by the shirt. "Did you take it, you worm?" she accused.

He shook his head. "No way. I want to win fair and square."

"I bet *they* took it!" Molly pointed her finger at Ashley and me. "They're jealous because you have your own TV show, Danielle. The Trenchcoat Twins only have a smelly dog."

That got me mad. "Clue is smart, not smelly," I said. "And if she was here, she'd find your stupid doubloons."

"Yeah. Probably in your cabin!" Molly said.

Ashley marched back down the hall. She flung open our cabin door. "You're welcome to check out our room," she told Danielle and Molly.

"Fine. We will." The two girls went into the cabin. Danielle walked straight to our dresser. "Look at *this*!" She gasped. She held up the silver globe.

Molly's jaw dropped. "That's the prize Susan and Karl lost."

They both turned and stared at us. Even Oliver looked shocked.

"Wait, we can explain," I began.

"Then explain it to Georgina!" Danielle fumed. "Because I'm telling!"

She and Molly stormed out.

"Tattletale!" Oliver called after them. Then he looked back at us. "How *did* you get that?" he asked.

Ashley sighed. "We'll tell you the whole story at breakfast," she said.

We told Oliver what happened last night and he believed our story. "Let's hope Georgina believes it," he added when we finished.

"But we can't tell Georgina," Ashley said. "What if she's the thief?"

Oliver threw up his hands. "Then let's go find our third prize," he said.

"Don't you think we should keep looking for the apple?" Ashley said.

I shook my head. "No, we should look for the thief," I suggested. "That way we'll find the apple."

Ashley unzipped her fanny pack. "Let's look at the clues and suspects again." She pulled out her pad. Then she reached into her pocket. "That's funny," she said, frowning. "The telescope's not here."

Oliver smacked his forehead. "Oh, no! Now we're *never* going to win."

"But I saw you put it in your pocket," I told Ashley.

Ahsley shrugged. "Maybe it fell out," she said.

"Let's walk back to the cabin," I said. "Maybe the telescope fell out on the way here."

We retraced our steps. Down the stairs. Down the hall. When we reached our cabin door, we stopped. No telescope.

"Maybe it's inside," Oliver said.

Ashley unlocked the door. She started to go in, but I blocked her with my arm. "Wait," I whispered. "I hear noises. Someone's in our cabin!"

We froze. Slowly I pushed open the door.

I peered into the cabin. I looked right, then left. Ashley breathed down my neck. Oliver tromped on my heels.

Nothing.

Had I just imagined those noises?

Then, all of a sudden, a funny movement

on the floor caught my eye.

I gasped.

Oliver sputtered.

My beach hat was moving across the floor—all by itself!

7

SCATTERED TREASURE

"Your beach hat is alive!" Oliver shrieked.

Ashley burst out laughing. "No it's not. It's Peter Pan!"

I blinked. My sister was right. The parrot's tail feathers were sticking out from under the hat.

We went into the cabin. Ashley plucked the hat from the floor. Peter Pan flew up and landed on the bunk bed ladder.

"What's he doing in here, anyway?" I asked.

"And how did he get in here?" Ashley said.

We both answered that question together. "Georgina!"

"I bet she was in here snooping again," I said. "Maybe she took the little telescope."

"Pieces of eight. We're rich. Pieces of eight," Peter Pan squawked.

Oliver snapped his fingers. "He keeps talking about money. Maybe he's trying to tell us that Georgina stole Danielle's gold coins!"

"Or maybe that's all he can say," Ashley put in.

"Aha! There you are, Peter." Georgina burst into our room. She wore a three-cornered hat with a feather, a white shirt, and a blue velvet vest. And she had a hook for a hand!

"Don't ask," Georgina said. "Captain Hook was my dad's idea." She held up her hook. Peter Pan flew down and perched on the silver curve. "How did you get in here?" Georgina asked him.

I eyed Georgina. "We were wondering the same thing."

Georgina shrugged. "I have no idea. He flew off as I was talking to my friend." Then she pointed behind me. "I bet *that's* how Peter got in your cabin."

I turned. She was pointing to the open window.

"Well, gotta go," Georgina said. "See you guys at three o'clock. Don't forget, that's the deadline for the hunt." Then she grabbed Peter Pan and left the room.

Ashley, Oliver, and I stared at one another. The deadline! And we still didn't have a single prize to hand in.

Ashley went over to check out the window. "Do you think the thief came in through here, too?" she asked.

"I can just see my sister trying to squeeze through," Oliver said. "She'd get stuck. Like a great big cork."

I grabbed Ashley's fanny pack. "Oliver's right. No one is that skinny, even a kid. Come on, let's get cracking on the third clue."

I took the clue from the fanny pack and handed it to Oliver. "Why don't you read it this time?"

Oliver unfolded the paper. Then he read out loud:

"On long voyages, even pirates had to work. Who used the sundial and compass? Pinpoint your answer—and your prize."

We all looked at one another. "Well, the sundial and compass both showed directions," Oliver said. "North, south, east, and west."

"Then the navigator used them," I said.

"Which means our prize must be in the

navigation room," Ashley added. "Let's go!"

We ran out the door, down the hall and up three flights of stairs. Then we jogged past the paradise pool.

It was hot and lots of kids were swimming. I spotted Trent playing water volleyball. Lizzie waved from the slide.

I sighed. "We could be swimming right now. We could be having fun."

Ashley grinned. "We *are* having fun, Mary-Kate. We're solving a mystery!"

Oliver led us past the shuffleboard players. One of the courts looked as if it had been sprinkled with gold.

"Hey, what's that?" I asked.

We went over to look. Gold doubloons were scattered everywhere.

"Those look like Molly and Danielle's coins," Oliver said. He stooped and picked one up.

"Stop right there!" someone ordered behind us.

I spun around. Molly and Danielle were pointing in our direction.

"We caught you!" Molly said.

"Just like my *Case of the Missing Chocolates* show," Danielle added. "The thieves led Gabby Gumshoe right to the stolen treasure."

"But we aren't thieves," I protested. "We found—"

"My own brother," Danielle went on, cutting me off. "A thief! How *could* you, Oliver? And we didn't even rat on you guys to Georgina. Yet."

Oliver jumped up. "How could *you* be so stupid, Danielle? We didn't take your doubloons."

"Or throw them all over the deck," Ashley added.

Molly dropped to her knees and started gathering the coins. "It doesn't matter anyway because now we have our two prizes."

Danielle waved a paper clue. "And we're

just about to find our third!"

I crossed my arms. "Gee, Danielle. Don't you think that's a little suspicious?"

"Huh?" She looked puzzled.

"You're the only team that isn't missing any prizes now," Ashley chimed in.

"Maybe *you* guys are the thieves!" I added. "Since you want to win so much."

Molly jumped up. She had coins clutched in both hands. "That is the dumbest thing I've ever heard."

Danielle linked arms with Molly. "Don't pay attention to them. Let's go find our last prize. So we can win!" They waltzed off.

"Hey, guys." Susan and Karl came up. "Did you ever find your missing prize?" Karl asked.

Ashley shook her head. "Nope. And we lost our second one, too. But we found this!" She gave them the silver globe.

"Cool!" Karl's eyes lit up. "Thanks."

"We found our second prize, a feather,"

Susan said. "So now we just have to find the last one."

"Well, good luck. Maybe you can beat Danielle and Molly," I told them.

Susan and Karl hurried off. So did we. We needed to find our last prize—or our team would end up with nothing!

We took the elevator up two flights. Then we hurried to find the navigation room.

We saw Captain Teach inside, hunched over a chart. Two other officers were working beside him.

But before we could even say hello, I froze.

A coat with captain's stripes was draped over the back of a chair. And in the pocket was our silver telescope.

Captain Teach had taken our second prize!

8

STOP THAT THIEF!

"**A**shley!" I whispered. I pointed at our telescope prize in the captain's coat pocket.

Ashley gasped. Then she motioned for me and Oliver to follow her from the room.

We found a quiet spot outside the door. Ashley and I told Oliver what we had seen.

"Captain Teach? A thief?" Oliver looked puzzled. Then his eyes grew wide. "Oh, no! Captain *Teach*. Edward Teach was *Blackbeard's* real name."

"Blackbeard? You mean the meanest,

most famous pirate of them all?" Ashley asked.

Oliver nodded. "You don't think the captain is a *real* pirate, do you?" He gulped.

I made a face. "Come on, Oliver. You've been reading too many pirate books."

Ashley nodded. "Right. Besides, the worst he could do is leave us on some desert island."

"That might be kind of fun," I added as a joke.

Nobody laughed.

We stepped back into the navigation room. The two sailors were still working. But Captain Teach was gone. So was his coat.

I sighed. "He must have gone out the other door."

Oliver groaned. "Now we have zero prizes."

"Not zero. One!" Ashley picked up a small compass from under the chair. The captain's coat had hidden it.

"We found our third prize!" Oliver cheered.

"But why would the captain take the telescope and not the compass?" I asked, puzzled.

Ashley was busy writing on her pad. "I don't know. But it's definitely very strange."

"Well, at least now we know who the culprit is," I said. "We caught Captain Teach red-handed."

"I'll bet he stole the prizes so he could give Georgina that trip," Oliver suggested.

"Let's go find him then," Ashley said.

My stomach growled. "Um, can we go have lunch first?" I asked. "We have two whole hours to find the captain before the deadline."

"Good idea," Oliver said. "After all, it's not like he's going to disappear."

Luckily, there was a huge lunch table set up on the sun deck. We made ourselves submarine sandwiches, and grabbed drinks and chips. Then we settled on lounge chairs. The sun was warm and bright.

Oliver and I ate. And ate. This mystery had made us both really hungry.

Ashley pulled out her pad again. "Here's the list of all the prizes that were stolen," she said. "Gold doubloons, silver telescope, silver globe, gold apple, gold treasure chest."

Suddenly I sat up. "Wait a minute," I said. "Now read the things that *weren't* stolen."

"Treasure map, feather, and little carved boat," Ashley read.

I wrinkled my brow.

"Mary-Kate?" Ashley tapped me on the leg with her pen. "What are you thinking?"

"All the objects that were taken are *shiny*. Why would Captain Teach take only shiny objects?" I asked.

"Because they're worth more?" Oliver guessed.

I shook my head. "The prizes aren't real gold or silver. They're just toys. Any *person* would know that."

Ashley and I jumped up at the same time and slapped palms.

"It's just like when we solved the *Mystery of the Hotel Who-Done-it*," Ashley said.

Oliver's gaze bounced from Ashley to me. "What's going on? Have you guys both lost it?"

"No. We just realized we've been thinking about the wrong suspects the whole time," I explained.

"Huh?" Oliver said.

"Come on! We've got a trap to set," Ashley said. "For a thief."

We all threw away our trash. Oliver grabbed a handful of cookies from the lunch table. Then Ashley and I sprinted across the deck. Oliver followed us, looking confused.

"We have only one hour left!" Ashley said breathlessly, looking at his watch.

We dashed to our cabin. "Shiny and bright," I muttered, sifting through my wooden box. "How about this?" I held up a gold necklace.

"Hey, that's mine!" Ashley protested.

"*What* are you guys doing?" Oliver asked throwing up his hands.

"Don't worry," I said. "Everything's under control." I tucked Ashley's necklace into my pocket. "Trust me."

We rushed upstairs to the ship's main level. In the entrance hall, I hung the necklace from a potted plant. The necklace twinkled in the light from the chandelier.

The three of us hid behind big potted plants. And waited. And waited.

"Our trap's not working," I whispered to Ashley.

"Shh," she said. "Be patient."

I checked my watch. It was two forty-five. "I can't be patient. The scavenger hunt will be over in fifteen minutes."

Then I heard a faint chattering noise. It got louder and louder. Then it turned into a rustling noise overhead. Ashley touched her finger to her lips. She pointed upward.

Calico Jack was in the palm tree. He jumped into a hanging basket. Then he reached down and snatched the necklace.

"*That's* our thief?" Oliver said.

"Yup. The only robber who could fit through a tiny window," I explained.

Jack chattered excitedly. Then he leaped onto the chandelier.

"Follow that monkey!" Ashley cried. "He'll lead us to the prizes!"

Jack jumped from the chandelier to the guest service's desk. From the desk onto a bell man's head. The bell man yelled. Then Jack dropped onto a baggage cart, just as a steward began to push it out of the room.

"Follow that cart!" I hollered.

We took off after the steward and the cart. But by the time we reached them, Jack was gone. I spotted a furry monkey tail whipping around a corner.

We raced down a hall filled with stores, and then down a flight of stairs. But when we reached the bottom, Jack had disappeared.

"We lost him!" I gasped.

"Now he's got my necklace, too," Ashley wailed.

I looked around. We were near the game room and arcade. "Wait. We're right near the lifeboats. Where we found Susan and Karl's prize."

Ashley snapped her fingers. "Could Jack be hiding the prizes in one of the lifeboats?"

I nodded. "It can't hurt to check." The three of us were off again.

We didn't have to search the lifeboats very long.

"There's that furry brown thief," Oliver whispered, pointing down the deck.

Jack swung up into a lifeboat. He ducked under the rubber tarp that covered it. Minutes later he popped out again. Then he dropped to the ground and loped off.

We ran to the lifeboat. Oliver and I boosted Ashley up. Slowly, she stuck her hand under the tarp.

Would we find the missing prizes?

9

A WINNING TEAM

"**W**hoa! Shiver me timbers!" Ashley exclaimed.

She pulled out her hand. It was filled with little gold and silver prizes!

I stared at all the glittering treasure. "Calico Jack sure lived up to his pirate name!" I said, laughing.

Oliver and I helped Ashley back down to the deck. "I think there may be some real jewelry in here, too." Ashley held out her hand. "Look."

"We'd better tell Captain Teach," I said. "*He* may not be a real pirate. But the ship's mascot definitely is!"

Oliver hunted through the loot. He whooped when he found the golden apple. "No telescope, though," he said. "It's probably still in the captain's pocket."

"There's my necklace." Ashley held it up. "Jack must have been the mysterious shadow we saw last night, Mary-Kate."

"Well, he's definitely our thief," I agreed. "Except a monkey can't write. So who left that scary warning about walking the plank?"

"Good question," Ashley said, frowning.

I checked my watch. It was after three o'clock. "Sorry, Oliver," I apologized. "We missed the deadline. I know how much you wanted to win."

For a second Oliver looked sad. Then he smiled. "Hey, that's okay. We solved a *real* mystery. And I had a great time, too."

We headed for Captain Kidd's Corner.

"Remember when Jack jumped into your arms?" I asked Ashley as we walked. "I bet he took the telescope from your pocket then."

"He reached into my pocket without me noticing?" Ashley replied.

"Why not? He swiped the globe from Karl's pocket." I shrugged. "He's a pretty clever thief."

We found Captain Teach in Captain Kidd's Corner. He was on the deck of the pirate ship, ready to award the grand prize. Georgina and the other teams were there.

I spotted Peter Pan perched on the rigging. Then I heard noisy chattering. Jack was hanging from a sail.

When Molly saw us coming, she gasped. "I *knew* they were the thieves. Look, they have all the missing prizes!"

"We can explain," I said quickly.

Ashley started to tell everybody what

happened. "We followed Calico Jack. And we found all this stuff in the lifeboat."

I looked at the other kids' faces. They looked angry and disappointed. I could tell they didn't believe us.

"*Screeech!*" Jack chattered angrily. He leaped from the sail and dropped onto Ashley's shoulder. His tiny paws snatched up a little gold pirate ship. Then he scampered off.

At first everyone was speechless.

Then Captain Teach burst out laughing. "By golly, mates. That rascal Jack *did* steal all those prizes!"

"Including the one he stuck in your pocket," I said to Captain Teach, pointing to the telescope.

Now everybody else started laughing, too. Except Molly and Danielle.

"Aren't you going to award Danielle and me the grand prize?" Molly said to the captain.

"We *were* the only team to find all three

prizes," Danielle pointed out.

"Not exactly," Captain Teach said. "The other teams found their prizes, too. But then Jack took them. We have no way of knowing who really won."

"We'll have to use the tiebreaker," Georgina said. "One more clue. And the team that solves it first will win the grand prize."

Georgina unfolded a piece of paper. She read aloud:

"'Anchor's Away!' Lift the answer to this clue and sail off with the prize!"

Georgina finished reading, and grinned. "This is a tough one," she told us.

I glanced around. Everybody looked totally puzzled. No one had a clue about the clue!

It was way too hard. And I was pretty sure I knew why. Georgina didn't want any of us to figure it out. *She* wanted to win the grand prize herself!

The other teams drifted off to figure out the answer. But I had a question for Captain Teach.

"What happens if no one solves the clue?" I asked him. "Does Georgina really get the trip to Adventure Island?" I shot the captain's daughter a suspicious look.

"Why, of course not," Captain Teach answered. "That wouldn't be fair."

Now it was Georgina's turn to look confused. "What are you talking about, Mary-Kate?"

"Mr. Banim told us that you went into our cabin," I explained. "Did you leave that scary message about walking the plank?"

Georgina nodded. "Sure. It was all part of the hunt. You know, to make things more piratelike. All the teams got one." Then she looked worried. "You didn't think that warning was real, did you?"

Ashley and I looked at each other. "Of course not," we said together. Then we slapped palms. "Case closed!"

"Psst." Oliver motioned Ashley and me over. "I know the answer to the tiebreaker clue!"

"You do?" Ashley whispered.

"Come on!" Oliver raced across the deck of the pirate ship to an open doorway. It led further down into the ship.

We followed Oliver to the middle of the ship. "The answer is...the capstan!" he told us. He pointed to a thick metal cylinder. It had long handles sticking out from it.

"*This* is the capstan," Oliver said. "The crew has to push it. When the capstan turns, it winds up a cable. The cable lifts up the anchor."

"So then the ship can set sail," Ashley said slowly.

"Anchors away!" I shouted. "We solved the clue!"

"Ah-ha!" Oliver bent down. "Look at this." He picked up a white envelope from the deck and ripped it open. Inside were four tickets.

We danced around the capstan. "Yo ho ho! We won! We really won!" we cheered.

Oliver handed us each a ticket. Then he led the way to the top deck. Everybody congratulated us.

Even Danielle and Molly.

"Well, Worm," Danielle said to Oliver. "I guess you're a better detective than I thought. Maybe you can be on my TV show."

Oliver grinned. "Cool!"

Ashley and I looked at each other. I knew we were thinking the same thing. We handed Oliver and Danielle our tickets.

"This way your whole family can go together," I said.

"Really?" Danielle looked excited. "Wow. You guys are the greatest. Maybe *you* two can be on my TV—"

"No, thanks!" Ashley and I quickly blurted.

"They're *real* detectives, remember?" Oliver told his sister. "But hey, maybe on our trip to Adventure Island we'll find a mystery to solve, too."

Danielle gave her brother a big smile. "That might be fun!" Then she turned to Molly. "And I'm going to ask my manager if you can come, too. After all, you're president of the Gabby Gumshoe Fan Club. That's a pretty important job."

Molly looked thrilled. "Gee, thanks, Danielle!" she said.

Ashley and I grinned at each other.

"Those guys will make a great detective team," I said as we all headed to a kids' party on the pool deck.

"You bet." Ashley put her arm around me. "Family detective teams are the best!"

Hi from both of us,

When our friend Patty invited us to her uncle's dude ranch, we gave the logical answer—yes! But the things that happened at the Logical I Ranch weren't very logical at all.

First we heard scary noises in the middle of the night. Then a terrible smell spread across the whole ranch. And to make things worse, we ruled out every person on our suspect list.

Could it be possible that a *person* wasn't behind all the trouble?

Want to find out the answer? Check out the next page for a sneak peek at *The New Adventures of Mary-Kate & Ashley: The Case of the Logical I Ranch.*

See you next time!

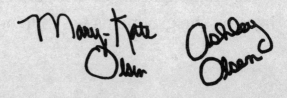

A sneak peek at our next mystery...

The Case Of The

LOGICAL I RANCH

It was getting pretty dark out on the corral. Ashley and I decided to head back to the ranch.

I pulled out my flashlight and shone it down at the ground so we could see where we were going.

"Hey, look!" I said. There were lots of footprints in the dust. Most were pointy-toed cowboy boot prints.

"They lead back to the ranch," Ashley added. "Let's follow them so we don't get lost."

My flashlight made a bouncing circle of light on the ground as we followed the trail of prints back to the ranch. Other than that, it was totally dark. And totally quiet.

"Th-this is kind of creepy," I whispered. I peered down at the ground. I wanted to make double sure we didn't lose the footprints.

Then I froze.

One step later, Ashley stopped, too. "What in the world is *that*?" She gasped.

There in the hard, dusty ground was the biggest footprint I had ever seen!

It wasn't a person's footprint. Not with claws like that.

"Oh my gosh!" I exclaimed. The huge track looked like it was made by...a dragon!